The Windhover

Windhover:
a small falcon that hovers in the air while hunting,
usually called a *kestrel* in the United States

To the school where the windhovers live. —A. B.

To Harry and Charlotte, and Class RK (1995/6) —C. B.

With thanks to the National Bird of Prey Centre, Newent, Gloucestershire

Text copyright © 1997 Alan Brown
Illustrations copyright © 1997 Christian Birmingham

First published in Great Britain by HarperCollins Publishers Ltd. in 1997
First U.S. edition 1997

Library of Congress Cataloging-in-Publication Data
Brown, Alan (Alan M.)
The windhover/written by Alan Brown; illustrated by Christian Birmingham.
p. cm.
Summary: A baby falcon is stolen from its nest in the school yard wall by a lonely boy,
who returns it when it will not eat and watches it take its first flight.
ISBN 0-15-201187-0
1. Falcons—Juvenile fiction. [1. Falcons—Fiction.]
I. Birmingham, Christian, ill. II. Title.
PZ10.3.B6915Wi 1997
[E]—dc21   96-48759

The text was set in Bembo.

A C E F D B

Printed and bound in Hong Kong

The *Windhover*

WRITTEN BY
ALAN BROWN

ILLUSTRATED BY *Christian Birmingham*

HARCOURT BRACE & COMPANY
San Diego   New York   London

When I open my eyes, the sky is the first thing I see, the wind is the first thing I feel. The blue sky strokes me with windy fingers, and the warm sun dries my wet feathers.

I hear chipping from the eggs close by my own broken shell. A hooked beak bursts through and gasps for air. There is more chipping, and soon I see a sticky wet head. A chick struggles out of its shell, and then another.

They are my brother and sister.

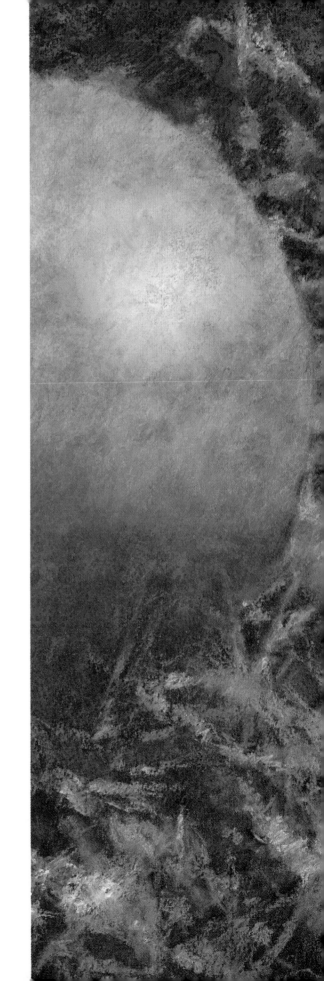

A great beating of wings thunders over us, and our mother arrives with food in her beak. It smells good and we screech, "Kee! Kee!" We are all hungry, but I am the biggest and the first to be fed.

   Our mother and father bring mice and shrews as fast as they can catch them. They tear them up for us to eat and we all grow fast, but I grow fastest.

We live on a ledge at the edge of the sky. Our roost is a hole high in the wall of a school. From here we can see across a playground and, farther away, green trees and a winding road.

We stretch our wings and beat them just like our parents. The children on the playground look up and point. "Look at the baby birds!" they cry. "Baby falcons!" They huddle together, their faces raised, except for one child who stands alone.

When the sack is opened I am dazzled by light. I try to fly but crash into strong bars and fall in a cloud of feathers. I am not yet strong enough. Where are the wind and the sky? Where are my home, my parents, my brother and sister? I am alone. Again I throw myself against the bars and again I fall.

"I want you for my own, my friend," a boy's voice says. "You're mine now." But I don't understand.

One evening, the school yard empty and the light weak in the sky, footsteps thud toward us. A dark shape looms and we screech, "Kee! Kee!" This creature has no musty bird smell—this is not our mother or father. We scramble to the back of the roost, and I peck and strike with my claws. Although we are all big, I am the biggest, and its two hands easily grab me. I am bundled into a soft darkness and taken from my home.

I remember this boy from the playground. Just as I am bigger than my brother and sister, so is he bigger than the other children. The other kids play together, but he is always alone.

He tries to coax me onto his hand, but I stay huddled in the corner. He brings food, but he does not tear it up and I cannot eat it. I become thin and weak. I call for my parents, "Kee! Kee!" but there is no answer.

The boy covers my head and I feel my feet being tied. I am carried in darkness to where I can feel the wind in my feathers. When the hood is pulled off, I beat my wings and try to fly.

"Dan Foster! You stole our falcon!" A girl has seen us.

"It's a windhover!" the boy says. "And it's mine."

"What's happened to him? He's so thin!" She comes near and leans over me.

"He's mine," the boy repeats. "But he's sick." His finger gently strokes my feathered head.

"You've got to put him back or he'll die," says the girl.

"I don't want him to die." The boy's voice is as soft as his finger on my head. "What should I do?"

"If you put him back," says the girl, "I promise not to tell."

Soon I hear familiar noises: laughter and shouting—the playground. I am nearly home! The children crowd around. "The falcon!" they call. The girl says, "Dan Foster found our falcon!" and the boy's face breaks into a broad smile.

I am home! My brother and sister hiss. They have grown bigger than me and do not seem to know me. But when I call "Kee! Kee!" they remember my sound and let me in. Then they walk to the ledge, beat their wings, and soar out over the playground.

The sky pulls at me with its windy fingers, ruffling my feathers, but I do not follow. I am alone on the ledge at the edge of the sky.

I hear the familiar thunder of great wings, and my mother swoops down to feed me. She remembers her first chick. At last I am safe. I eat and I eat.

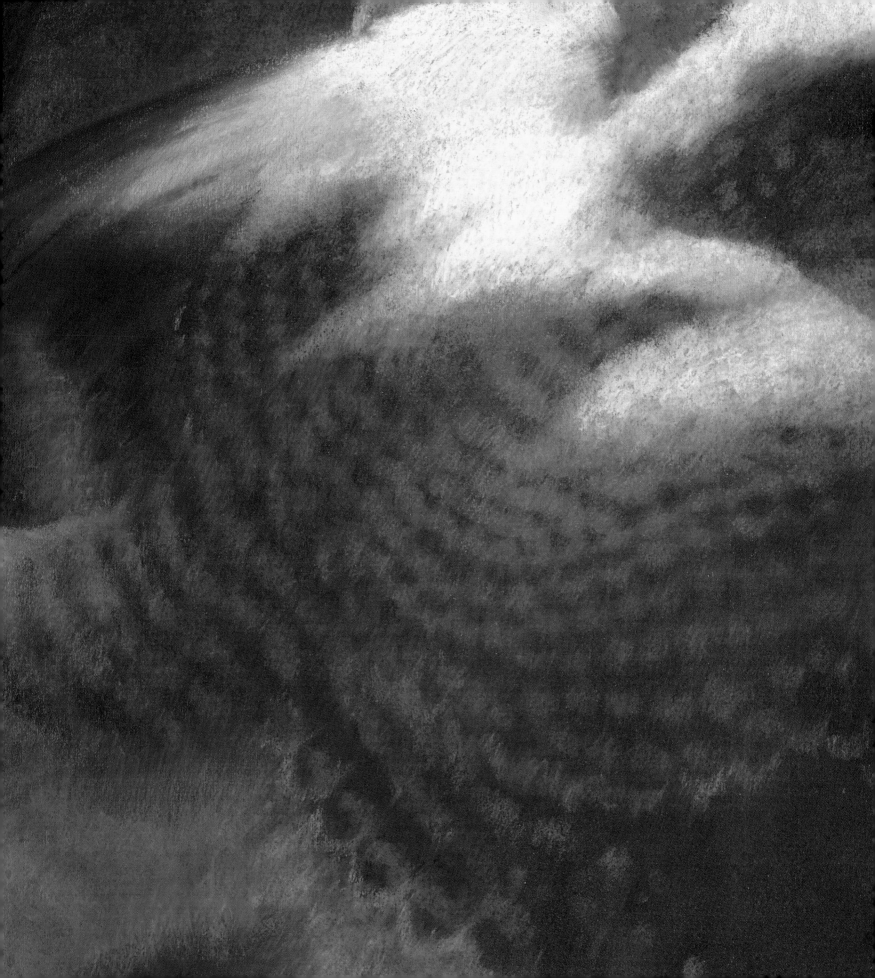

Days pass. Soon my wings are smooth and strong. My fluffy feathers are gone, but I stay on the ledge at the edge of the sky. I do not want to leave home again. The children look up and call out, "The falcon is afraid to fly!"

My father alights on a pole across the playground. He has a shrew in his beak for me. I am hungry and call, "Kee! Kee!" but he stays on the pole.

My brother lands in a tree and also calls for the food. He will reach it before I do unless I leave my safe home and fly. I softly beat my wings.

Suddenly I feel the thickness of the air and the wind lifting me. I launch myself off the ledge and the air carries me up and across the yard to the pole. I can fly! I snatch the shrew from my father's beak, and I hear the children laugh and cheer in the playground below.

The sky and the wind are my friends. I flutter my wings to float high in the blue sky above the school. My sharp eyes search for mice as I hover on the wind.

Far below, I see the boy. The girl stands beside him. The two look up and point. "It's your windhover!" the girl shouts.

"*Our* windhover," he replies.